I Would Tuck You In

Sarah Asper-Smith

Illustrations by Mitchell Watley

SASQUATCH BOOKS
SEATTLE

For our parents with love
—SAS & MW

Manufactured in China by C&C Offset Printing Co. Ltd. Shenzhen,
Guangdong Province, in July 2017

Published by Sasquatch Books
19 18 17   11 10 9 8

Editor: Susan Roxborough
Project editor: Michelle Hope Anderson
Illustrations: Mitchell Watley
Design: Anna Goldstein

Library of Congress Cataloging-in-Publication Data is available.

ISBN-13: 978-1-57061-844-4

Sasquatch Books
1904 Third Avenue, Suite 710
Seattle, WA 98101
(206) 467-4300
www.sasquatchbooks.com
custserv@sasquatchbooks.com

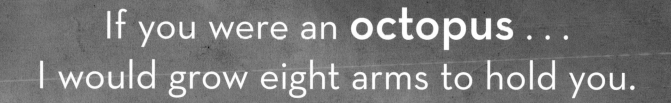

If you were an **octopus** . . .
I would grow eight arms to hold you.

To avoid predators, the common octopus can lose an arm and regrow it later on.

If you were a
brown bear . . .

To bulk up for their winter sleep, brown bears may eat as much as ninety pounds of food per day.

I would snuggle next to
you all winter long.

If you were a
little brown bat . . .

The little brown bat uses sound at night to find its way
in the dark and capture mosquitoes to eat.

I would find you on
the darkest of nights.

If you were a
rufous hummingbird . . .

my heart would beat 1,000
times per minute for you.

Hummingbirds are the smallest birds in the world, but their hearts can beat up to 1,500 times per minute.

If you were a
porcupine . . .

I would still want to
hold you close.

Porcupines protect themselves with their 30,000 quills, but unlike
what some people think, they can't shoot them at predators.

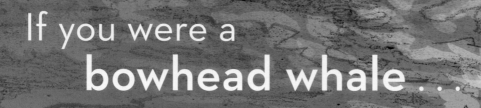

If you were a
bowhead whale . . .

I would break through
Arctic ice to find you.

To create a breathing hole, bowhead whales can
break through ice that is twelve inches thick.

If you were an
Arctic tern . . .

I would fly to the ends
of the Earth with you.

Arctic terns have the longest migration route of all birds, sometimes traveling all the way from the North Pole to the South Pole.

If you were a
caribou . . .

Caribou migrate thousands of miles in large herds,
and produce a clicking sound when they walk.

I would hear you coming from miles and miles away with a clickety, click, click!

If you were a
humpback whale . . .

Because humpback whales don't have vocal chords, the songs that
they sing come from pressing air through their nasal passage.

I would sing a song
to soothe you.

If you were a
musk ox . . .

I would huddle close to you
and keep you warm.

Musk oxen conserve heat by clustering
together when it is cold and windy.

If you were a
boreal owl ...

I would stay up all night
and tell you stories.

Boreal owls are nocturnal, which means that they sleep during the day and look for food at night.

If you were a **walrus** . . .

I would carry you on my back
while swimming in the sea.

Walrus calves will frequently ride on their mother's
backs while swimming and while on land.

If you were a
sea otter . . .

Sea otters rest in kelp beds, wrapping themselves up
in the seaweed ribbons to keep from floating away.

I would tuck you into
a kelp forest bed.

If you were a
snowshoe hare . . .

Snowshoe hares change from brown in the summer to white in the winter for camouflage (to blend in with their surroundings).

I would change my colors
to play hide and seek with you.

If you were a **hermit crab** . . .

I would watch you grow into
each new home you found.

Hermit crabs live in abandoned snail shells and find bigger and bigger homes to live in as they grow.

But no matter what, I will always love you for who you are.